Little Boy With Three Names
Stories of Taos Pueblo

By
ANN NOLAN CLARK

Illustrations by
TONITA LUJAN
of Taos Pueblo

Ancient City Press
Santa Fe, New Mexico

International Standard Book Number:
ISBN 0-941270-59-9
Library of Congress Catalogue Number:
89-081747

Book design by Mary Powell
Front cover illustration and design by Ellen Fox

10 9 8 7 6 5 4 3

Contents

Little Boy With Three Names

Little-Joe, the First Name

ALL THE MORNING noises of Taos were sounding together, telling the people that a new day was waiting for them.

Little-Joe opened one black eye. Sleepily he looked up at the long, straight, white aspen poles which made a ceiling overhead. "Where am I?" he asked himself. "What is this place around me?"

His brown hand came out from underneath the bed cover. It went feeling about on the wool-filled pad beneath him. "This is not my white bed. Where is my white bed and all the other white beds in this dormitory?"

Little-Joe rolled over on his stomach. His head came out from the covers. It turned this way and that way. "I am just like a turtle looking out from my shell," he told himself, and laughed himself awake. Both black eyes were open now. They lighted up the slender brown face of the little Indian boy.

He knew where he was, now that he was all awake. This was his mother's house. This was his bed on the floor of the family sleeping room. Beneath him was the mattress of soft wool that once had covered his father's sheep. He saw the good earth floor, hard-packed by walking feet.

Little-Joe stretched and stretched. Today summer began and he was in Taos again.

In the outer room he heard the soft footsteps of his mother as she moved about cooking breakfast for her family. He heard his older sister, Iao, playing with the baby. Iao's voice made little running sounds like water. The baby's laughter answered like the splash of a stone in the creek.

"I am the lazy one, to lie sleeping while my family move about me," thought Little-Joe. "But then, they will forgive me. I am new here. I have just come back from school."

Little-Joe sat up. He looked around for clothes to wear. Last night he had placed his school shoes side by side near the corner fireplace. He had neatly folded his blue shirt and blue overalls and placed them on a stool beside his shoes. Down there, at the school, they had taught him that way. But now his clothes were gone. Deerskin moccasins stood where the school shoes had been. A calico shirt and beaded leggings were beside them. The little blue shirt and overalls and the two school shoes were gone. There was no place in all this room for school clothes to feel at home. Everything here was new and strange to the little boy who had lived at boarding school.

Everything here was Indian, for this place was Taos. It was the beginning of summer.

Little Taos boys live in Taos in summer.

Tso'u, the Second Name

LITTLE-JOE PUT on his calico shirt. It was yellow. It had red flowers and blue flowers on it. He rubbed them with his thumb and fingers. They would not come off. They were in the goods. The shirt was long. It was an Indian shirt. It flapped against him as he walked.

Little-Joe turned himself about, but all he could see was long yellow shirt. He thought he did not like it. "I know my school shirt so much better," he said to his Indian shirt. "It does not flap against me. It stays inside."

Little-Joe put on his leggings. Down each side they had a beaded band. Last summer he had been too small for leggings. These looked strange, but they were pretty. Then the little boy put on the deerskin moccasins. These were right. His small toes felt at home in them. They could feel the cool hard earth floor of his mother's house. They could make his feet walk lightly and swiftly without noise.

Little-Joe stood up. He was dressed for the day.

He stood in the center of the family sleeping room of his mother's house. A trail of sunlight came from the small high window to the hard earth floor. He watched the sun trail, running his fingers through the dancing flecks of light. He listened. There were no bells. There were no children marching. There were no school sounds of any kind. A dog barked. Far away a Taos man was singing. The music of the song made a narrow trail through the stillness like the trail the sunlight made through the shadows.

Slowly Little-Joe turned toward the door. Slowly he opened it and went through into the outer room where his mother was getting breakfast. His mother's fat, white deerskin boots rubbed together as she walked. They made a soft little swishing noise. Her bright blue dress was fresh and clean. A woven red belt tied her waist in. Her black hair shone against the brownness of her slender face. She looked like a tall blue flower standing there. She smiled at her son. "Tso'u, my little hunter, slept hard," she told him.

His sister, Iao, called to him, "Tso'u, come know our baby. Come here by the fire. Your place is waiting for you." Little-Joe walked slowly to his sister. He felt very much alone and a little afraid. Always at school they had called him Little-Joe. Now he was not Little-Joe any longer. The Little-Joe name had been put away with his school clothes. Now he was Tso'u.

Tso'u meant little hunter. It was the Indian name for the Indian boy who was now where Little-Joe had been.

Mother brought breakfast.

Baby looked at Tso'u, but she held to her sister. Tso'u went to the open door. He walked big, taking high steps so that no one would know that he felt alone and a little afraid.

Outside was Taos. The morning sun was smiling through the blue. Fat clouds promised rains to the new-planted fields. They promised rains as a little wind herded them along. The high blue mountains were getting ready for the day. They were lifting their heads from the night blanket of mists.

The houses of Taos stood high around the plaza. Their mud walls had been rounded and smoothed by the hands of Taos women. Their doorways and windows and ceilings were of aspen and pine. Taos men had brought the aspen and pine down from the mountains.

These were the houses, the homes of Taos, which had been built by the hands of Taos people. They did not know a little boy who had become used to wooden floors and walls of red brick. They did not call to him. They did not welcome him. They let him stand among them alone and afraid.

Mother called that breakfast was ready to be eaten. Father came in. He was very tall. His black hair was twisted into two long rolls and bound with ribbons and hung in front. His long leggings were like Tso'u's short ones. His white sheet was folded tightly about his hips. His Indian shirt was yellow too, with red flowers and blue flowers on it.

Tso'u looked at his tall father. He saw his father's kind face. He saw his father's friendly eyes. He wished that his own hair was long and bound with ribbons. He wished that he wore a white sheet folded tightly about his hips.

Suddenly Tso'u felt alone no longer. This was his father near him. He felt not at all afraid. He felt Indian. In his toes and in his fingers he felt Indian. In his heart he felt Indian. He was Tso'u, little hunter of Taos.

Tso'u laughed and his father laughed with him. They sat down together on the floor and mother brought breakfast. They were two Taos men, eating together. Baby crawled over to share their food. Iao smiled happily. She and her mother sat down to eat with them.

"Perhaps I, too, can wear a sheet this summer?" asked Tso'u. "I think so," his father answered him.

Everything was friendly and right. This was Taos and the beginning of summer. Tso'u felt at home again. He liked his Indian name, "Little Hunter." He went running out of his mother's house and into the plaza.

Little Taos boys were playing there. They ran shouting through the river. They jumped from the bridge and splashed water high over the willows. They raced on the north side and on the south side of the pueblo. Dogs barked and ran around them in circles. Babies toddled out of doors and sat down to watch the wild playing of the little boys.

Men stood on the housetops. They stood silent and still, wrapped in their snow-white sheets. They were watching. They were waiting. Always in Taos there are men on the housetops watching and waiting. Tso'u saw them while he was playing. He knew that when he was older he would be told why Taos men always stood on the housetops watching and waiting for something.

Mothers and little girls went up and down ladders and in and out of doors. Big girls, home from school, called to one another across the plaza. Tso'u said to them, "You are to call me Little Hunter now. My father and I, we have put the Little-Joe name away."

Grandfathers slept in the sun. Grandmothers sat looking at the high blue mountains and sang little songs to bright-eyed babies. Men came, bringing their horses to water. They stopped to play with the babies and speak to the grandmothers. They made jokes with the little boys. Then they went on to their fields.

Tso'u climbed to his mother's housetop. He, too, was waiting. Soon Pablo would come looking for him. Pablo was his best friend, even though he had more years than Tso'u had, and was taller. Pablo was his dearest clan brother. Always, until last year, they had been together. Last year Pablo had been brought home from boarding school. The old men of Taos had needed Pablo for learning things. They had chosen him. When he grew to be a man he would be one of the holders of Taos wisdom. Now he must be a little apart from other boys. He must learn to endure more

Men stood on the housetops.

pain, to fast longer, to be quicker and braver than his playmates. He must teach his body to be strong. he must teach his heart to be good. He must make ready. He had been chosen a keeper of knowledge.

Tso'u felt a little sorry for Pablo. He felt, also, a little in awe and a little envious of his dearest clan brother. As he stood on his mother's housetop, he thought of things that he would say to Pablo. "I will say to Pablo," planned Tso'u, "I will say to him many things." To himself he talked softly, "Pablo, for many days I have been to school. I can talk the English. I can read the books. My hair has been cut by the barber."

Just then Tso'u began climbing down the ladder. Pablo was running toward him across the plaza. Speaking at the same time they called one another. "Tso'u, I bring you a little yellow dog." "Pablo, soon my hair will be long like yours."

The little boys came running together. The little yellow dog came running between them. He licked Tso'u's face. He licked Pablo's face. The friends touched hands again. Pablo spoke shyly, "In Taos

Pablo was running toward him across the plaza.

they call me Pachole. I am known by that name here." Tso'u said, "But I think of you as Pablo." The taller boy put his hand on his friend's shoulder. "Any way you think, I like it."

The little yellow dog barked at them. "And this one here, we will call Yellow-dog," laughed Pablo. Tso'u laughed with him. Both school and secret learnings were forgotten. They were best friends. They were clan brothers. They went off to the river together with Yellow-dog frisking between them.

Jose la Cruz, the Third Name

YELLOW-DOG WAS in charge. Tso'u was scolding him. Yellow- dog put his head on his paws and looked up at Tso'u. "You are a bad dog," Tso'u was telling him. "I am ashamed of you. Always, when there are visitors, when there are other people in automobiles, you scratch yourself. Only today I hear them laugh at you. They are telling each other that the yellow one has fleas. What of it? Need you scratch yourself before the automobiles of visitors? Why do you not go behind my mother's oven to chase your fleas?''

Little Yellow-dog looked very sad as he lay in the sun with his head between his paws. He did not know why he was being scolded. He could not answer Tso'u. He could just look at him.

After a while Yellow-dog went to find a shady spot and Tso'u went to get one of his father's ponies. He wished a horse belonged to him. He wished that he and Pachole could go riding their horses together.

Pachole was busy. This day he had no time for playing. Tso'u and his father's horse went off toward Palo Flechado Hill. Tso'u went in search of the great pine tree there. This tree was very tall. It was big around. It was old. Pachole had promised his friend that some day he would tell him the Taos story of the tree. Tso'u liked to listen to stories. he was lonesome for Pachole. He was lonesome for Yellow-dog, too. He was wishing that Yellow-dog was with him. He felt sorry, now, that he had scolded Yellow-dog. "If I had not scolded my little dog," he said to his father's horse, "he would be with me now, instead of sitting in the shade by my mother's house." The pony twitched his ears and swished his tail and jogged along. "I must bring meat back for my good dog's supper," thought Tso'u. "I must be friends with my dog again."

The sun had hidden its face in a cloud. Tso'u did not notice. The horse turned its head sideways. It grew uneasy. Perhaps it felt that a storm was coming, but Tso'u noticed nothing. He was thinking of Yellowdog and the Palo Flechado pine tree.

Black rain clouds gathered on the tops of the tallest pine trees. The world lighted with angry yellow.

Tso'u looked up from thinking. He saw that he must go home. He turned his father's horse about upon the trail. He was high on the mountainside. The trail was narrow. At one side was a bare rock cliff and below was the deep tree-filled canyon.

Now the horse acted afraid. Wind howled in the trees. An arrow of lightning tore a hole in the sky and shot to earth in a line of blue fire. It struck a tall pine which burst into flame. At once the wind took the fire and carried it along.

Tso'u knew what he must do. He must go quickly on his father's horse for men to come to stop the fire. Trees were blazing by the sides of the trail, but he must ride beneath them. He must ride through the wind that was sweeping the fire along.

Tso'u unwound his sheet from his hips and with it covered his face and head and shoulders. Only his eyes peered out from the white folds. He lay flat on his horse's back. He shouted, "Run, run, my pony! Run, my pony!"

Smoke was thick. It hung heavy about him and crept in beneath his sheet and clothing. It choked his throat. It blinded his eyes. It rose up from the fire in the undergrowth. Blazing branches dropped on every side. A great tree crashed across the trail behind the frightened horse.

They ran on and on. It seemed forever to the boy as they raced through the blazing pines. But at last they reached the meadow country. Here the storm had not touched, nor had the wind swept it with wings of fire. Everything was as usual, quiet and happy in the summer sun. But Tso'u did not stop. He kept on and on. He shouted over and over, "Run, run, my pony! Run!"

They saw a rider ahead of them on the trail through the pasture. It was Father Paul, the priest from the neighboring village of Ranchos. Tso'u called and pointed behind him. A thin line of smoke curled up from the mountains.

Father Paul understood without words. At once he turned off on the trail back to Ranchos. He raced his horse to get help. No one man can fight a forest fire.

Tso'u kept on toward the pueblo. He passed men working in the fields. To each one he pointed backwards. They saw the thin line of smoke far up on the mountains. Old men and young men ran for their horses. Some headed for the mountains and others back to the pueblo. Each one shouted to the next one and pointed backward. The men going to the pueblo called as they raced toward it. The women came running from their houses. They, too, understood without words, what was happening in the mountains.

They knew what that call meant. They came running to meet the riders. They brought buckets and shovels for the men to take back up the trail. They would need them to fight the fire.

When Tso'u reached the plaza he met Pachole there. Pachole had his own big, black horse and he was leading a fresh one for Tso'u. Yellow-dog was there, too. He started to go with the boys, but mother called him back. She told him, "No. Your place is to watch the house."

Tso'u and Pachole went back up the trail. Soon they caught up with some of the men. Father Paul came riding from Ranchos and with him were the Mexican farmers. Men came, also, from the neighboring town.

They rode fast up the trail to meet the oncoming forest fire.

All night the men worked, fighting the fire. They dug ditches at the end of the fire line. They beat the fire with blankets and sacks and green branches. They smothered the fire with dirt. They buried the creeping flames with dampened earth. They drenched the coals with water.

All night the boys helped the fighting men. They climbed down the canyon sides for water. They climbed back carefully so as not to spill a drop.

They grew tired. Their eyes pained from smoke. Their shoulders and arms ached from carrying the heavy buckets of water. Their faces and hands and feet were scratched and bleeding. Their hair was scorched from heat.

When the sun came up it saw a blackened forest. Burned, charred stumps stood where once tall trees had grown.

But the fire was dead. Not one tiny flame was left.

The tired men rode down the home trail. They rode into the Taos pueblo. Father Paul and the Mexicans from Ranchos rode into the Taos pueblo with the Indians. The other men from their town rode with them, too. They went straight to the little Taos church to pray. They went to give thanks that the forest fire had been put out.

Then Father Paul talked to them. He told them

about the little one who rode through the blazing trees to get help. Father Paul said, "Jose la Cruz, come forward my son, that all may know the small boy whom our great Father chose as messenger."

Tso'u stood by his father's side. He did not know Jose la Cruz. His father had to tell him. "You are Jose la Cruz, my Tso'u. That is your church name."

Uncle came to the back of the church where father and Tso'u were standing. He took Tso'u by the hand and led him before all the people. He led him to the priest. There before all the men Father Paul blessed the little Indian boy. He said, "God our Father, we thank You for the bravery of Jose la Cruz."

There stood the little Taos boy. There stood the little boy who had three names, one for school and one for home and one for church, Little-Joe, Tso'u, Jose la Cruz.

Father sat down on the wall ledge seat.

Going to Blue Lake

Advice

DAYS GREW LONG and hot and lazy. Little boys shouted and played on the rooftops of the houses. They played along the narrow passage-ways between the houses. They played in the hidden patio gardens. Grandfathers made them bows and arrows and rabbit sticks and little drums. They taught them songs and dance steps. They told them stories.

Father brought home two new, white sheets. One was large and one was small. Father put the large one on, wrapping it about his hips, folding it in wide, neat folds. Tso'u put the small one on, twisting himself about to see if he looked like a real man. He did. At least he thought he did.

Father sat down on the wall-ledge seat. He stood his small boy between his knees and talked to him of many things that boys should know. He told his son about the work of growing up to be a man. He told his son how a man's trail through life should go. He said, "A man must keep his footsteps in the trail that he has chosen."

He told the boy about Taos sacred lake. How the mountains held and hid it. How the snows of winter fed it. How the sky leaned tenderly over it and gave blue color to its still, deep waters. With a stick father drew in the sand. He made a line for the trail to sacred Blue Lake. He showed how the trail went up and up and up through the mountains. Father said, "Some day when you are older, you will go there with the men of your village. You will go there to learn things that only an Indian may know."

Tso'u listened to all that his father told him. He felt happy and strong and good. He felt "growing-up." After a little while of thinking he whispered low to his father, "I think that lake is calling me to come. I want to go there."

Now it was his father's turn for thinking. All was quiet and still while father sat, and thought, with his small boy between his knees. At last he answered Tso'u. He said, "I can see no reason why you and

Pachole can not make that journey. The trail is long, but you are strong." Then father thought some more. He told his little boy to go out in the plaza and play with the other boys. He told him, "Tomorrow will be an important day." But that was all that he would say, just, "Wait for tomorrow."

Tso'u went to the plaza to play a little, and to wait for the slow coming of tomorrow. Sun Old Man moved by on lazy feet. But a last he put himself away behind the mountains.

Night came. . .and sleep. Then it was morning. It was yesterday's tomorrow.

The New Horse

FATHER WAS GOING to Community Pasture. Tso'u and Pachole were going to Community Pasture. Yellow-dog was going, too. Community Pasture belongs to all the people together. There they pasture their horses.

They were very quiet as they went along. They were thinking. Father walked first, then Pachole,

Father walked first, then Pachole, then Tso'u.

then Tso'u. Yellow-dog came last. He looked as if he were thinking, too.

This was the important day. This was the day that Tso'u was to choose his horse. Any horse that he could catch from his father's herd was to be his horse.

Tso'u walked quickly, thinking his own thoughts. "I will catch my father's fastest horse," he thought. "My father's strongest horse, my father's biggest horse will be mine. Then when I am a great hunter my horse will go with me. Me and my horse, we will go together. We will ride out into the new morning. To the Great Plains of my Grandfather's father my horse will take me hunting. Who knows? There may yet be buffalo that only a horse of swift feet can find."

So planned the little boy as he took quick steps, thinking big thoughts on his way to the Community Pasture.

When they reached the Pasture, father took down the bars of the gate. Father went in first, then Pachole, then Tso'u. Last of all, Yellow-dog went in through the bars of the gate.

The grass was like a blanket underfoot. It was

short where the horses had eaten it. Clear water filled the creek bed. Tiny hummingbirds darted here and there among the wild flowers. There were many horses, more horses than Tso'u could count, although he had been to school.

Father pointed out a horse that belonged to him. He pointed to another and another. "This one," he said, "is a fast running horse. The one over there is a good trail horse. This one drinking needs to be handled gently. The one by the tallest cottonwood tree will bring good money in the market at Ranchos."

Father gave Tso'u a rope. "Go, my son. Bring back your first horse," he said to his little boy.

Tso'u took the rope. He was not afraid. He knew how to throw a rope. Yellow-dog was the one to know how well Tso'u could throw a rope.

The small boy walked among the horses. Their heads turned toward him. They looked at him. Some got ready to run away. The rest began to eat again. They had no time for such a little boy. Tso'u walked along. His deerskin moccasins made no marks on the stiff, short grass of the pasture. He held his rope

The pony put its soft nose in Tso'u's hands.

ready. He turned his eyes this way and that way. Pachole held Yellow-dog. Nothing must disturb Tso'u in catching his first horse.

Then Tso'u stopped. He had seen his horse. It was a white pony with four brown stocking feet. It had friendly eyes. Tso'u's heart beat high, for he knew his pony. Of all the horses in the Community Pasture he had found the one pony that must belong to him. Tso'u walked swiftly. Would his pony know him? Would it be glad to belong to him?

Tso'u stepped closer and closer. The pony raised its head. It looked at Tso'u. Its eyes were asking questions. Tso'u dropped his rope. He stretched out his hands in welcome. The pony seemed to know him. It put its soft nose in Tso'u's hands. It poked him gently in the shoulder. "My horse," Tso'u whispered. "My horse. You and I together."

Father and Pachole left. They went to look for their own horses in the Community Pasture. Yellow-dog waited for Tso'u. His red tongue hung out of the side of his mouth. His eyes were shining as though he was laughing. He was waiting for Tso'u and his white pony to ride out into the morning together.

Getting Ready for Blue Lake

SEVERAL DAYS WENT by. They were long-lasting days. They were slow-moving days. But at last it was time to make ready for the journey to Blue Lake.

Iao made stacks of tortillas. She kneaded and patted and pounded small balls of wheat flour dough. She kneaded and patted and pounded small balls of blue cornmeal dough. She clapped a ball of dough between her hands. She clapped it this way and that way and this way and made the dough ball thin and round and flat and big. When a dough ball was as thin and round and flat as a plate she threw it down on a hot, flat stone in the fireplace. When it browned she turned it quickly, Iao never burned her fingers when she made tortillas.

The stack of white and spotted brown tortillas grew and grew. Iao was making them for Tso'u and Pachole to take to the Blue Lake in the morning.

Mother made wheat flour bread. She made long loaves of wheat flour dough and placed them side by side on a board in the sunshine. She made a cedar-fire in her out-of-door oven. When it had burned to coal she swept it clean with a cornhusk broom. She took the loaves of wheat flour dough from the board and slid them into the hot, clean oven. Then she closed the oven door with a big, flat stone and left the bread to bake. She left it there to rise to light and fluffy bigness and to get a sweet brown-color crust.

The whole plaza became filled with the fresh, clean smell of baking bread that Tso'u and Pachole would take with them to Blue Lake in the morning.

Grandfather brought out a bag of dried deer meat. Pachole's mother made Indian cookies.

Tso'u and Pachole and Yellow-dog were in everyone's way. They felt important, but they did not get much done. Pachole had a gun, but Tso'u had to be content with his little bow and arrow and his sling-shot.

The day was very long, but at last it ended. Night came and the stars and sleep.

Then once again it was yesterday's tomorrow.

In the morning, early, Pachole came to Tso'u's house. He looked very tall on his big black horse. He

Mother made a cedar wood fire in her out-of-door oven.

looked very proud. His white sheet covered his head and was thrown grandly over his shoulder.

Tso'u brought his pony from the pasture. He used a blanket for a saddle. He used a rope for a bridle. Pachole tied the bags of food to his saddle ties. They were ready.

The boys and Yellow-dog were ready for their journey to Blue Lake.

The sky was red with sunrise. Early morning mist hung low over the plaza. Taos people were just wakening as the boys rode over the bridge of the little river and between the houses and out of the village.

Journey to Blue Lake

YELLOW-DOG WAS glad to be going. He would run ahead on the trail and then come running back to see if all was well with the boys and horses. White Pony went first. He did not like to follow on the trail. That was the one thing he was always cross about. He wanted to be first. Pachole's black horse did not care and

Pachole looked very tall on his big black horse.

Pachole was glad for his little, best friend to ride ahead of him.

The trail led away from the summer ranches and the fields and the gardens. For a long way it led through pasture and meadow land. The wild flowers were thick and bright. They lay stretched in a gay blanket of dancing yellow and white and green. Higher up the flowers were blue to match the mountains and the sky.

Then the trail led into the mountains. Soon it became steep. Morning mist hung heavy. The air was wet and cold. Evergreens closed in, putting their tall heads together. The trail was wet with mountain night rains.

The boys crossed a little stream. Their horses stopped long to drink slowly, to look around and to drink again. Birds scolded and sang. Yellow-dog chased a gray squirrel.

The trail wound through a canyon. On each side rose high walls of rock. The trail was narrow here. Pine trees crowded it. The boys rode carefully so that branches would not scratch them. Spanish moss

The trail led into the mountains.

hung from the pine tree needles. Tso'u called back to Pachole, "That Spanish moss makes the trees look like Spanish ladies trailing their lace mantillas." Pachole laughed at this. He said, "To me they look like Mexican traders, old ones with dirty gray whiskers."

The trail grew narrower and darker. It was shadow-filled. High up on the face of the canyon walls were deep cracks and caves and patches of dull green moss.

The boys heard water dripping, dripping. They could not see it. They heard birds calling and the wind in the pine trees. Tso'u's teeth chattered. He thought of the warm sun in the pueblo plaza.

The trail turned and began climbing the mountains. It went up and up. It zigzagged and twisted. Soon the dark canyon was below them. White Pony stumbled on a loose stone and for a moment Tso'u was frightened. He saw the treetops below him. He saw between them, down, down to the floor of the canyon. He hoped he had not cried out in fright. He turned quickly to look at Pachole but Pachole was looking at trail marks and Indian signs. If Tso'u had cried out in fright, at least Pachole had not heard him. Tso'u was glad. Pachole would not like having to be ashamed of his friend.

White Pony regained his footing and the boys rode slowly upward.

Yellow-dog sat down to rest. His sides went in and out with panting. As usual, his red tongue was hanging out. He was tired.

Pachole slid from his horse. "I think that we had better lead our horses here. The trail is so steep." Tso'u was glad to slide down from White Pony's back. He was glad to put his feet solidly on the rocky trail.

The mist began to thin and let the sunshine through. Tso'u liked the feeling of the warm sun on his back and his shoulders. He felt happy and strong and brave again.

He sang a Taos song as he rode along. White Pony twitched one ear. He was listening. Perhaps he liked it. Yellow-dog came back. He stood in the middle of the trail and looked at Tso'u. He was listening, too. He gave two short, sharp barks. Pachole laughed at

White Pony and at Yellow-dog. Then he began to sing with Tso'u.

This is the song that the Taos boys sang as their horses carried them up the trail to Blue Lake.

·· GOING TO BLUE LAKE SONG ··

First note in each measure strongly accented.

E-ya hay-ya hay-ya hay-yo hay-ya hay-yo hay-ya hay-ya hay – yo hay – yo

E-ya hay-ya hay-ya hay-yo hay-ya hay-yo hay-ya hay-yo hay – – e – – – ya

E-ya Wayhay hay-ya hay-yo-a way-yo hay ya-hay yo-hay a-ya hay yo

Noontime found the boys high in a mountain meadow. The thick grass was knee high and dotted with wild flowers. The horses ate, and switched their tails lazily. The boys were hungry. Their noon lunch of cold tortillas and dried deer meat tasted good to them. They drank cold mountain water. The water came straight down from the snow banks above them. Pachole called it star water. The boys gathered blueberries and hunted on the sunny slopes for wild, sweet, strawberries. Then they lay on their backs in the deep grass and looked up through the trees at the warm blue sky so far above them.

Yellow-dog chased squirrels and chipmunks. Up and down and around and around Yellow-dog went digging and barking and running after squirrels and chipmunks. Finally he came back and looked down at Tso'u. He licked Tso'u's face as if he were begging him to start on the trail again. He would run off a little way and run back and jump at Tso'u and bark little excited barks.

The boys understood him. They knew what Yellow-dog wanted to do. Lazily they got up and caught their horses. They started on the trail again.

Soon they were riding through an aspen grove. The aspen trees were slender and white and tall. Their bright green leaves danced with the white sunlight, making quivering patterns of light and shade. The aspen had grown as the winds had told them to grow. Some were straight and close together. Others had become broken and fallen and bent. They had been twisted and turned by the angry winds of winter storms. But now their bright leaves were dancing in the sunshine and the pain of winter was forgotten.

The boys' trail circled here, for they wanted to descend to a mountain meadow for night camp. Tso'u's father had drawn the trail carefully with his stick. He had told them where to turn and how to find the down-trail fork. Father had told them that there was a Mexican sheepherder with his flocks in this meadow and that they must stay the night with him.

A summer shower came up and clouds hid the sun. The boys wrapped their sheets tightly about them, but the cold water drops came through. The trail grew wet and slippery. Pachole rode ahead now, looking for trail signs, and White Pony was restless and ill tempered.

The mountains had a wet, musty smell. The trees grew together and were not friendly. Everything was strange. The rain beat down with a steady, dreary pounding. This was not the gentle rain of valley lands where the green fingers of growing things reached up and up thirstily for pattering water. This was mountain rain, angry and loud.

The boys rode on through the downpour. White Pony fretted, but Pachole kept the lead. He must, for he had to make sure of the trail signs.

As suddenly as it began, the rain stopped. The sun pushed the clouds away and came smiling through. Gray raindrops on the Spanish moss turned to silver starlets. Everything was right again, happy and warm. The trail circled a high point and the boys rested and looked down. It was still raining down in the valley. But they were above the clouds now. They were up in the warm sunshine, looking down at a raining world beneath them.

Steam rose from the wet ground and their horses' wet sides. Sheep smell came thickly through the clean, rain-washed air. Yellow-dog barked. The boys turned their ponies and soon were in the meadow with the sheepherder and his flock.

The herder was glad to see them. He was Manuel from Ranchos. Pachole knew him. They talked together in Spanish.

The boys were soon in the meadow with the sheepherder.

The herder's dog came to meet Yellow-dog. Both dogs growled, low and very fierce. The hair on their backs rose up. They growled some more, but they did not fight. They let it be known, though, that they were not afraid to fight.

Yellow-dog sniffed at the herder and at the herder's sheep. He walked stiff-legged and looked very cross and very brave. Tso'u was proud of the way that Yellow-dog looked. He was glad that Yellow-dog just looked like fighting and did not fight. That way was best. Tso'u did not want his good dog hurt.

Soon the herder's supper fire was started. It was little. Its smoke was blue and it curled thinly upward. It smelled sweet and sharp in the cool, damp air. Coffee boiled in its blackened can. The herder warmed some goat meat stew. The boys shared their bread and cookies. They drank rich, yellow goat's milk and coffee.

Night comes quickly in the mountains. The boys were glad to roll themselves in the herder's dry sheep skins and move close to the fire. Tso'u was tired. The sheep huddled together, their heads turned inward. They could sleep. They were safe with the herder's dog there to protect them.

Night sounds filled the air. Far away a mountain lion screamed.

Tso'u reached his hand out and touched Yellow-dog. He whispered to him, "It is good to have you, Yellow-dog, close here beside me."

Everyone slept.

When Tso'u wakened again, Pachole was shaking him. It still was night, but the herder was getting breakfast. The boys had planned this early start, for they wanted to see sunrise over Blue Lake.

While they were eating breakfast, the stars began to fade. Dull gray light filled the night sky.

The boys hurried and before long were on the trail again. Their horses were rested and so they walked fast. It was very cold. The sky became lighter. Everything was so still, the whole world was sleeping.

Pachole slipped from his horse and pointed. They had come to an over-hanging cliff. Tso'u looked down.

Above them were snow peaks, red with sunrise. Below them in the green of the trees, in a cup in the mountains, was Blue Lake. Beautiful and still, Blue Lake, like a live thing, rested there.

The sun rose higher and the mountains wakened with the singing of the birds. Hundreds of birds' songs filled the air. Flashes of bird colors flew among the trees, but the lake below was quiet and deep and blue.

After a while the boys led their ponies downward. They went softly between the trees to the edge of the lake. Tso'u went as close to the blue waters as he could get.

Pachole came to stand beside him. His big, black horse looked over his shoulder. Pachole spoke shyly. "That is my name, Blue Water, Pachole. Did you know it?" Tso'u looked up at this tall, dear brother. "Of all the names, that is the best for you," he answered.

Blue Lake was still. The wind did not ruffle it. The mountains hid it. The snow peaks fed it. The sky leaned tenderly over it.

The boys had made the journey because Tso'u had felt it calling. They had come alone into the mountains. They had come over a trail that was narrow and steep. They had come over a trail that was hard to find, that was slippery with rain. They were alone in the heart of the mountains where only deer and bear and mountain lion lived. They were alone, two little boys and their horses and their dog, looking at Blue Lake. Beautiful Blue Lake that only an Indian can get to know.

They did not know that they had done a brave thing in going into the mountains alone. They did not know that many boys could not have done it. They only knew that here they were, looking into the heart of a lake that kept forever the secrets of their people.

Many more times they would go to Blue Lake, but never would they forget this first time when they had gone alone into the mountains and found the sacred lake that is hidden away from the eyes of most men.

The boys stayed until the sun was straight overhead and the shadows hugged the tree trunks. Then they started for home. They did not talk. They had no need for words.

They rode down the mountains to Taos. The wild flowers nodded to them as they passed by. The sun warmed them. The wind sang to them. The houses of Taos welcomed them. They had been to Blue Lake.

Taos Long-Summer

July

SUMMER PASSED SLOWLY in Taos. There were long days and happy star-lit nights.

There were days of irrigating. The boys turned the slow- moving water from Mother-ditch into the little ditches to feed the thirsty plants of fields and gardens.

Pachole always was patient. He never grew tired of waiting until each plant had its share to drink. He taught Tso'u to think long thoughts while the lazy water moved along, wetting the thirsty earth.

There were days and days of wood gathering. Out-of-doors ovens are greedy for the dry branches of the mountain slopes.

Pachole taught Tso'u how to tie the sticks into bundles that fit the back with comfort. He taught him how to save his breath in the high places, how to breathe in climbing upward, how to bend his knees in

There were days and days of wood gathering.

walking down hill. He showed his smaller brother how feet must keep their balance when walking over rolling stones.

The boys dug yucca weed for its fibers. They dug its root for soap. They gathered wild tea and guaco and juniper berries for their mothers to use. They rubbed their faces with the leaves of aspen to keep the wind and sun from burning them. Tso'u helped Iao to dry rose petals. All Taos girls have pillows stuffed with dried rose petals.

Pachole showed Tso'u the plants that were used for snake bite and for medicines. Pachole knew them all. He was rich in learning.

The boys found the tracks of mountain lion and wildcat. They found a packrat's nest with its sweet little pinon nuts. One noon they rested at the bedded-down place of a bear and her cubs. They saw the deep scratchings high up on the trunk of a near-by pine tree where the mother bear had sharpened her great claws.

Once they saw a deer looking at them through the aspen trees. They smoked a prairie dog family out of its underground hole. They saw an owl on a tree. They shot a chicken hawk, flying.

Pachole taught Tso'u how to use his gun. He taught him how to oil and clean it. Father promised that next summer Tso'u should own a gun.

At night Pachole would point out the evening star. He would join in the evening dancing. The old men would listen and nod. Their choice had been wise. They were pleased.

The winds and the shadows, the moon and the stars, were as books to Pachole. He was being taught to read them.

The long days of summer moved slowly.

In the early mornings all the boys of the village ran races. Sometimes they ran in great numbers. Other times they ran in small groups of three and four. They liked racing.

Tso'u was a swift runner. Pachole could teach him little about running. He ran swiftly and lightly like a young antelope. His feet scarcely touched the ground. "I win all the races," he told his mother. "It is because of the moccasins of deerskin which you made for me. I am a great runner among the boys."

His mother was not pleased with him. "Spend your time in thanking your moccasins," she told him, "and not in bragging."

Tso'u went out and sat upon the ladder of his mother's house. He was sorry that his mother had found it wise to scold him.

In the evenings the people danced. In the houses and in the plaza they danced. Sometimes the women and girls did the circle dance or the scalp dance or did dances borrowed from the Plains Indians. The men gathered around them and sang and beat the drum.

Sometimes the men and boys danced. They danced the fun dances and the dances of the summer season.

Old men taught the young boys the right steps and the words of the songs. Tso'u and Pachole learned the hoop dance. Uncle sang for them. Over and over they did the hoop dance, for the people liked to watch them.

When the moon was high the young men gathered at the little river which ran through the plaza. The young men of the south plaza stood on the

The men gathered around and sang and beat the drum.

south bank of the little river. The young men of the north plaza stood on the north bank of the little river. They joined their singing. They sang love songs to the girls of the village. The wrapped themselves in their white sheets and sang songs in Taos and in English. They made the music for their singing with their drums.

··TAOS LOVE SONG.··

He ya he ya he ya he ya O he ei hi   He ya he ya he ya he ya O he ei hi   ya

He ya o e ya he ya   he ya o ya he··· a··o   O ya hey o ya   e ya hi i ··· i··   ya

He ya o e ya he ya   he ya o ya he   a··a   a ya he ya o ha   e o hi··i··· i··

Sometimes Tso'u and Pachole went with the young men to the little river. They sat on the bridge with the other boys. They must know all the songs when their time came for singing. They wrapped their white sheets about them and learned the words and the music.

August came to Taos, bringing purple asters and

They wrapped themselves in white sheets and sang songs.

guaco and yellow golden-rod and chamisa and sun
flowers. The wheat was cut and threshed. It was win-
nowed, washed and dried, and stored away. Winter
apples hung heavily from the trees in the orchards.
The store-rooms smelled of dried apricots and wild
plums. Melons in braided strips and chili in scarlet
strings hung from vigas. Corn was piled high before
every door while the people husked it.

Going to Gallup

AT THE VERY last of the month the men made ready for
their yearly trip to the Indian Ceremonial at Gallup.

At the Indian Ceremonial in Gallup many Indian
tribes meet to feast and dance together. Non-Indian
people come from many lands to see the Indians,
their beautiful costumes and dances. Non-Indians
like the Ceremonial almost as much as the Indians do.

The old men met to choose the dancers from
Taos. They spent a long time at their meeting. Differ-
ent members talked long and with much thought.
They wanted to choose good dancers.

At last they decided on ten old men and ten young men and two boys. These were to go to the Ceremonial, they said.

The next night the old men had another meeting. This meeting was to decide on the dances to be given at the Cermonial. This meeting took a long time, too. The members thought long and made long speeches. They wanted to decide on the best fun dances to give, for religious dances may not be given away from the pueblo. At last this meeting was finished also. They had decided that one was to be the hoop dance. Pachole and Tso'u were to give it. They were the boys who had been chosen to go with the ten old men and the ten young men.

For many days and many nights the people made ready to go to the Indian Ceremonial at Gallup. The dancers did their steps over and over and over agin. The chorus of singers practiced their songs. Every step and every word must be just right. Taos people have no Indian books in which are written their songs and dances; they must remember their songs and dances from year to year. Old men teach the boys. These boys must learn perfectly, for some day

Tso'u's grandmother made him new leggings.

their work will be to teach the new boys in the pueblo.

Tso'u's Grandmother made him new beaded leggings. His Grandfather made him beaded moccasins. His Father made him little fantail feathers and fan arm feathers. His Mother made him a new red shirt.Pachole, too, had new leggings and moccasins and feather ornaments. His shirt was green.

At last the day of starting came. The ten old men and the ten young men and the two boys were ready. All the dance costumes, the feathers and flutes, and the gourd rattles and drums were made into great blanket-covered bundles. The men and the boys were dressed in their best shirts and leggings and moccasins. Their sheets were as white as snow. Their black hair had been freshly washed with yucca and bound with new ribbons.

They were ready. They waited in the plaza and talked and laughed with the other Taos people.

The Trailway bus came for them. It stopped by the bridge of the little river. All the little boys and the dogs and the babies and all the little girls crowded around it. All the Grandmothers and Grandfathers

They waited in the plaza.

crowded around it. All the school girls and school boys crowded around it. The fathers and mothers came to their doorways.

The many blanket bundles of dance costumes and feathers and flutes and gourd rattles and drums were put on top of the bus. The ten old men got inside the bus. The ten young men got inside the bus. The two boys got in, too. They leaned out the windows and waved goodby. The people in the plaza waved goodby.

The Taos dancers for the Indian Ceremonial were off to the town of Gallup.

The blue mountains and the green fields were left behind as the big Trailway bus went down the hill of Rio Grande Canyon.

All the hours of the day they traveled. The Rio Grande grew large. It did not look like the little river of Taos Canyon. It did not look like itself at all. By and by the big bus crossed it on a white stone bridge. Tso'u wondered what the waters, running so quietly under the bridge, thought of these Taos people so far from home.

The big bus traveled quickly. It went through the

towns of non-Indians with funny houses with pointed tops. Sometimes the bus stopped at the towns and the young men got off to walk up and down beside it. Pachole got off, too, but Tso'u stayed on with the old men. He was afraid the bus might go and leave him. Pachole called for him to come, but Tso'u said, "No. These old men might need me."

Soon they were riding again, smoothly and quickly. They passed through yellow sand country, so different from the fields of home. They came to the red-rock country of the Navajos. Uncle began to sing and one by one all the old men and all the young men joined in his song. Shadows grew long.

Far away was the Mesa Encantada. It looked like a cloud of darkest blue that had fallen down. Uncle pointed it out and said that some other kind of Indians lived near it. Their village was called Acoma. Uncle explained that they were Pueblo Indians, too, but not like the Taos people.

Late in the evening they reached Gallup, the town of the Indian Ceremonial. It was a town of little hills and streets and sidewalks and houses of non-Indian people.

They came to the red rock country of the Navajos.

Ceremonial

THE BIG BUS did not stop in the town. It went on through the streets out to the Ceremonial grounds.

Neither Tso'u nor Pachole had been here before. They were excited. The Taos men left the bus and went into the long-house. Long-house was a long adobe building which the non-Indians of Gallup had built for the Pueblo Indians to use during Ceremonial time.

Pachole and Tso'u left their blanket bundles at long-house and then they went outside with Uncle. Uncle took them visiting.

First, they visited the other Pueblo Indians who were also staying at long-house. Then Uncle took them over to the Navajo camp. The Navajo Indians were staying in round, earth and log houses called hogans. The two boys had heard of hogans in the stories of the days-of-the-old which Taos old men had told them, but they had not seen these round houses before.

The Apaches camped near their covered wagons

The Navajo Indians were staying in round, earth and log houses called "hogans."

and slept in them, under the canvas tops. The Apaches' horses looked tall and black in the shadows of the camp fires.

Plains Indians had put their tipis in a circle. Tso'u had seen tipis many times. The Plains Indians made teasing jokes with the Taos boys. They pretended to be afraid of such warlike visitors. They said, "Look at these Navajos," and "Here are those warriors from Oklahoma." But all the time they knew that the boys were the Taos people.

The shelters of the California Indians were made of grass. Uncle said that was so they could be taken down quickly. Then Uncle laughed as if he had made a good joke. The California Indians would not talk. They had things to do.

The Utes were fat, both men and women. The Comanches were tall, like Taos people.

All the people whom the boys visited were Indians. But all of them spoke different languages. Their houses were not alike. Their camp fires looked different. The people themselves did not look alike.

Tso'u and Pachole were surprised. They talked

about this to Uncle on the way back to the long-house and the supper fires of the Taos men.

At the campfire supper there was buffalo meat and bread and coffee for everyone. Tso'u had not tasted buffalo meat before, but he knew how it should taste. His grandfather had told him. He said to the man at the barbecue pit, "I would like the meat from the hump part. It is sweeter there." All the Indians laughed. Even Pachole laughed. Tso'u did not like it. He took his bread and meat and sat within the shadows.

After the Indians had eaten they made ready for dancing. Pachole rebound his long hair, and Tso'u made his in a war-like roach as his grandfather had taught him to do it. They put on their arm feathers and their fantail feathers. They put on their dance moccasins. They got their willow hoops and Uncle's drum.

Then they joined the long, long line of Indians. Those who lived nearer and had come on horseback were at the head of the line. They rode their horses forward, slowly. Slowly they rode them into the great oval plaza of the Indian Ceremonial grounds. Slowly they walked them around the plaza and out again into the soft blackness of the night shadows. Then the line of men on foot moved forward. They moved forward into the Ceremonial plaza. There three of the biggest campfires that Tso'u had ever seen were burning. Their great logs crackled and blazed, sending showers of little sparks up into the night sky. All the tribes of Indians were singing their own songs. Some men made little dancing steps and other men stepped high into the light of the fire flames.

At the front side of the dancing space there were seats. They were high like the houses of Taos. Many people were sitting there. You could see their faces in the darkness. You could hear their hands moving. You could feel their eyes looking at you. You could feel them liking you.

At the back of the dancing space were the standing Indians and their horses and their wagons and their shelters and their camp fires.

The stars were crowded close together and they were hanging low.

The line moved on before the seats of the people. Tso'u made dancing steps. He was not afraid. He could feel his heart beats in his fingers and in his toes. He knew that his arm feathers and his fantail feathers were shining in the firelight. He whispered to Pachole, "I am riding White Pony over the high places. The clouds are at my feet. Rain falls below me."

Now all the Indians were in the Ceremonial dancing plaza. They stopped walking. They grouped themselves at the back of the plaza. Then the different tribes danced their dances. Their chorus of singers sang for them and made them music with their rattles and drums and little bells.

Tso'u watched. He liked it.

Soon it was time for Taos dancing. All the faces out in the darkness were looking. The camp fires flamed. Uncle sang the hoop dance song. Pachole and Tso'u danced. They turned their hoops this way and that way and made their bodies go through them, like the music of Uncle's singing. They made their bodies like water, pouring through the hoops in a flashing

Uncle sang the hoop dance song.

stream. They stepped lightly, lifting their feet as the words of the song lifted high in the air.

Then it was finished. The hoop dance was finished. All the dances were finished.

The Indians went back to their campfires. Tired ones went to sleep in their blankets, but the old ones sang the stars to bed and sun to a new day.

For three days and three nights the Indians sang and danced and feasted together. On the morning of the fourth day the Ceremonial was over.

The Indians went back to their homes. On horseback and in wagons, in cars, on trains and buses, the Indians went home.

Ceremonial was over.

Back to School

SEPTEMBER DAYS CAME over the mountains of Taos bringing cool evening winds and cooler night frosts. Morning mists were slow in rising.

One night the whole Taos world turned yellow.

Summer was finished. It was time again for boarding school.

Mother brought out the blue shirt and the blue overalls and the school shoes. Tso'u put them on. They were little for him. The shoes hurt him. They felt like cages to the slender brown feet that had been so free. Iao put his Indian clothes away. Father cut short the hair that tried so hard to grow long.

White Pony was put with Father's horses in the Community Pasture. Yellow-dog was to stay with Pachole, who had one more year at Taos before he would go back to school.

All the other little Indians were getting ready for boarding school. All deerskin moccasins and the Indian names had been put away. The red church surplices had been folded away with the yellowed church book where the Spanish church names were written.

Just boarding school names and boarding school clothes are used in Taos in September. Tso'u was now Little-Joe again.

Robert and Josephine and John and Mary stood

Mother brought out the blue shirt.

beside Little- Joe in the plaza and waited for the yellow school bus to come up the hill of Rio Grande Canyon.

"Pachole, I will send you a store collar for Yellow-dog."

"Mother, if you would like it, I can learn to carve a bed for you." "Here comes the school bus."

"Goodby." "Goodby."

Taos summer is over. Little-Joe is going back to school.